Beauty
AND THE
BEAST

Illustrated by Seo Kim

BONNEY
PRESS

KU-470-335

Published by Bonney Press,
an imprint of Hinkler Books Pty Ltd
45–55 Fairchild Street
Heatherton Victoria 3202 Australia
www.hinkler.com.au

BONNEY
PRESS

© Hinkler Books Pty Ltd 2016

Illustration: Seo Kim
Text: Katie Hewat
Design: Paul Scott and Pooja Desai
Editorial: Emily Murray

All rights reserved. No part of this publication may be reproduced, stored
in a retrieval system, or transmitted in any way or by any means, electronic,
mechanical, photocopying, recording or otherwise, without the prior written
permission of Hinkler Books Pty Ltd.

ISBN: 978 1 4889 0591 9

Printed and bound in China

Beauty
AND THE
BEAST

There once lived a rich merchant who had three beautiful daughters. One winter's day, as the merchant was about to set off upon a long journey, he asked his daughters, 'What gifts would you like me to bring you when I return?'

As expected, the two eldest asked for silk gowns and jewels.
But when his youngest daughter, Beauty, asked only for his safe
return, the merchant insisted that she choose a gift as a reward for
being such a loving daughter.

Beauty thought for a moment and said, 'I would be so grateful if you
could bring me a single rose. I do love them so.'

Several weeks later, as the merchant was travelling home, the sky turned **dark** and snow began to fall, freezing him to the bone. Chilling winds swept the land and the merchant knew he must find shelter or perish.

Finally, he saw some lights shining in the distance. Cold and shivering, he made his way along the road until he reached a majestic castle.

Much to his surprise, the merchant found one of the castle doors open.
Through the door he could see the warm glow of a hearty fire, and
was drawn inside. He called out as he entered, but there was no reply.

Once inside, the merchant found a long dining table set for one. He hesitantly sat down but soon started feasting on hot stew, roasted duck and vegetables. Then the merchant sat in a big chair beside the fire and soon fell fast asleep.

The next morning, the merchant awoke to find a warm blanket draped over him and a fine suit laid out for him to wear. On the dining table was a magnificent breakfast for one.

The merchant ate his breakfast, dressed in the suit, and called out a *'thank-you!'* to whatever magical being had taken him in for the night. As he went outside to fetch his horse, the merchant noticed a gate leading to a garden.

Remembering Beauty's request, he entered the garden to find row upon row of blossoming roses. He chose a perfect pink bloom, and tore it from the bush.

Suddenly there was a great howl, and the merchant looked up to see a terrible creature rushing towards him.

'How *dare* you!' yelled the Beast. 'I have given you everything you could need, and still you steal from me.'

The merchant felt both scared and sorry. 'Please forgive me,' he begged, 'I only took the rose for my daughter, who loves them so.'

But the Beast would not forgive him so easily. The following morning, he sent the merchant home with a horrible demand. The merchant feared the Beast's punishment if he did not do as he was told, and left the castle with a **heavy** heart.

When the merchant arrived home, he told his daughters what had transpired on his journey. With great regret, he repeated the Beast's demand. 'One of you must go to live with the Beast of your own free will,' he said sadly, 'or I am doomed.'

'*I* will go, Papa,' said Beauty. The merchant was distraught at the idea, but Beauty wouldn't have it any other way. So, one week later, they set out for the Beast's castle.

When they arrived at the castle, Beauty was awed by its charm. Again, the door was open and the table was set with a wonderful feast.

As they finished their meal, a terrible **ROAR** came from the top of the stairs and the Beast appeared. Beauty was terrified of the hideous creature, but was determined not to let her father down.

The Beast asked if she had come willingly, and Beauty bravely replied, 'Yes.'

'I am pleased,' growled the Beast.

The next morning, after her father tearfully departed, Beauty sat upon the steps, weeping. After a time though, she became curious and began to explore the castle. Upstairs, she found a room with her name on the door.

Inside, there were fine furnishings, clothes, jewels, books and even a harp. Beauty soon understood that she would want for nothing while this was her home.

That night, as Beauty went down to dinner, the Beast met her on the stairway. 'May I join you?' he asked in his **gruff,** *growly* voice.

'Of course,' replied Beauty. 'This is your home after all.'

During the meal, Beauty found that the Beast was surprisingly well-mannered.

Afterwards, the Beast asked Beauty, 'Will you marry me?' Beauty simply shook her head.

The following months passed quickly. Beauty spent her days exploring the castle and wandering in the garden.

Every night she talked and laughed with the Beast over dinner. Beauty soon found that these meals were the best parts of her day.

But, at the end of each evening, when the Beast would
ask Beauty to marry him, Beauty would sadly tell him no.

'Beast, you are my *dearest* friend,' she told him one night.
'Can't you be happy with that?'

'I love you with all of my heart,' said the Beast,
'But I can only be happy if you promise to stay here forever!'

Beauty was happy at the castle, but she missed her father; so she made a deal with the Beast. 'If you permit me to go home to my family for one month, I will return to the castle forever', she said.

'Please come back to me, Beauty,' the Beast said. **'I cannot live without you.'**

The next day, Beauty returned home to her father, who had become ill with worry. He was very glad to have her home and soon returned to full health.

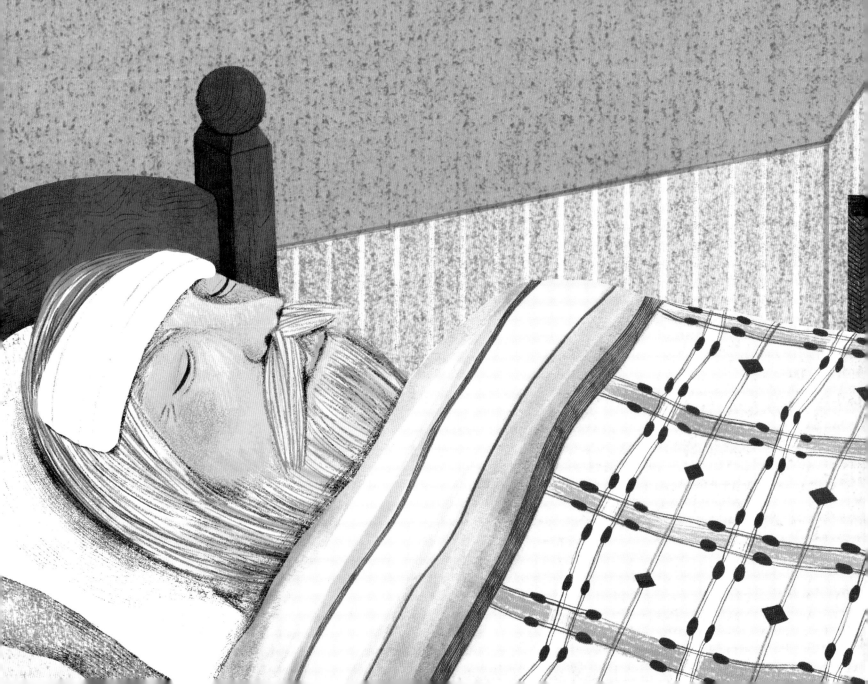

Time passed by so quickly that Beauty barely noticed when a month had passed. Then one night she had a terrible dream where she saw the Beast lying in the garden, gravely ill. The next morning she travelled back to the castle as quickly as she could.

When she arrived, she searched the castle but could find no sign of the Beast. Terrified, she ran to the garden, where she found him lying on the ground – she rushed to his side.

'I'm sorry I was gone so long,' Beauty whispered, 'I didn't realise how much I loved you until it was too late. *I will marry you*, Beast, if you'll **just wake up!'**

Then, a miraculous thing happened. The Beast began to shake, and soon there was no longer a creature lying before Beauty, but a handsome prince.

Beauty was shocked and asked where her Beast had gone, but the prince replied, 'I am right here!' He told Beauty how an evil witch had cast a spell on him that could only be broken by *true love*.

Beauty and the prince were married the next day. A grand carriage was sent to fetch Beauty's father and sisters, and the king and queen soon arrived to attend the wedding.

The king and queen were so grateful to Beauty for breaking their son's curse that they made her father a great lord, and they all lived *happily ever after*.